var + mint   ('vär-mənt) *n. informal:* an irritating or obnoxious person or animal. [dialect variant of *vermin*]

To Emily and Tyler, from Daddy
M. C.

HELEN would like to thank Marc for turning her few words into an epic and also Alison for her steadfast support.
Most of all, Helen would like to thank Mike for tirelessly championing VARMINTS over the years, for pulling everything together,
and for turning gray skies blue more often than he should have to. ("Can we do another one?")

MARC would like to thank his partner, Karine, as well as Helen, Mike, and Alison for their unfaltering patience, encouragement, and enthusiasm,
and Sue, Pam, and Philip for their support, guidance, and chance taking over the years.

Text copyright © 2007 by Helen Ward
Illustrations copyright © 2007 by Marc Craste

All rights reserved. No part of this book may be reproduced, transmitted, or stored in an information retrieval system in any form or by any means, graphic,
electronic, or mechanical, including photocopying, taping, and recording, without prior written permission from the publisher.

First U.S. edition 2008

Library of Congress Cataloging-in-Publication Data is available.

Library of Congress Catalog Card Number pending

ISBN 978-0-7636-3796-5

10 9 8 7 6 5 4 3 2 1

Printed in China

This book was typeset in Rats Regular.
The illustrations were done in Adobe Photoshop.
This book is made with paper from a sustainable forest.

Candlewick Press
2067 Massachusetts Avenue
Cambridge, Massachusetts 02140

visit us at www.candlewick.com

VARMINTS

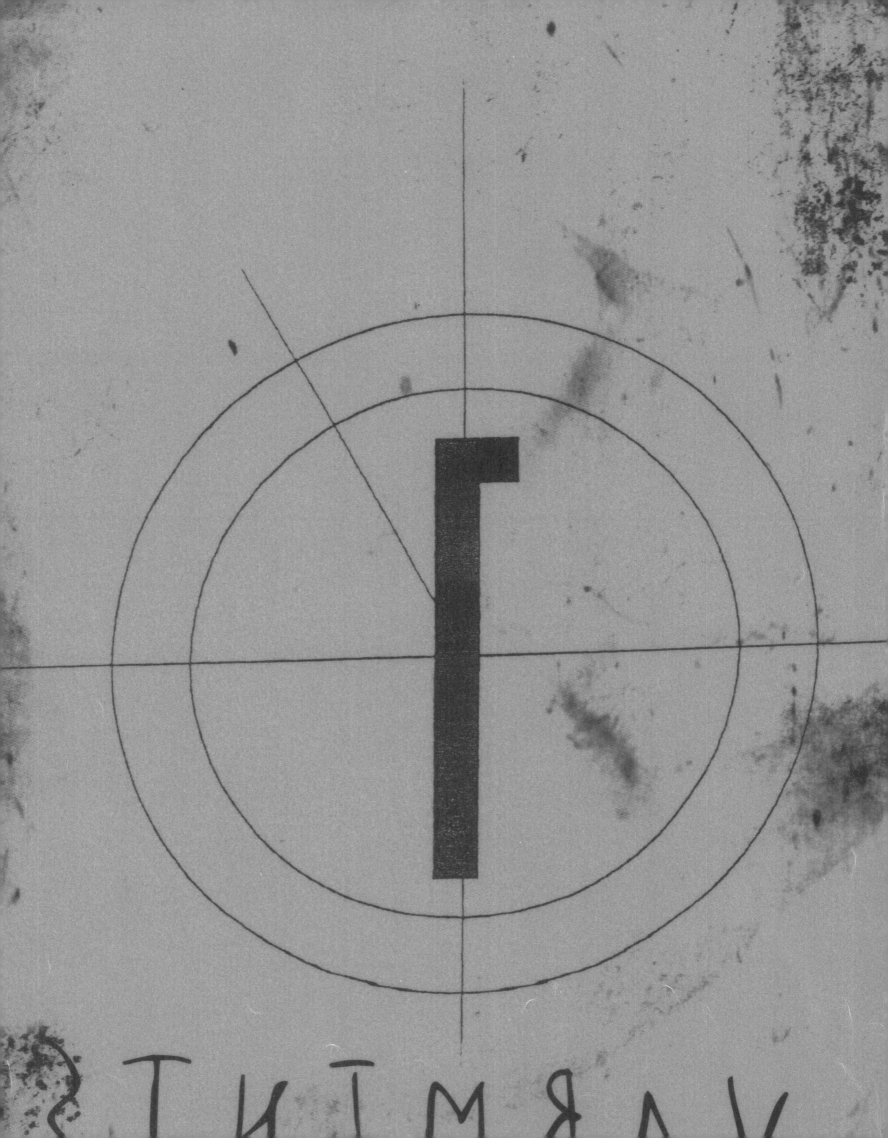

varmints helen ward illustrated by marc craste

CANDLEWICK PRESS
CAMBRIDGE, MASSACHUSETTS

ONCE,
the only sounds to be heard were the bees,

the whispering wind in the wiry grass...

and the song of birds in the high blue sky.

These gentle sounds
  touched and warmed the hearts of those FEW
    who paused and cared to listen.

Then one day OTHERS came,
and the sound of bees was lost.

Their tall buildings
scratched the sky where birds once sang.

Those gentle sounds faded and were gone.

Every day
there were MORE OTHERS,

making
MORE NOISE

and listening less . . .

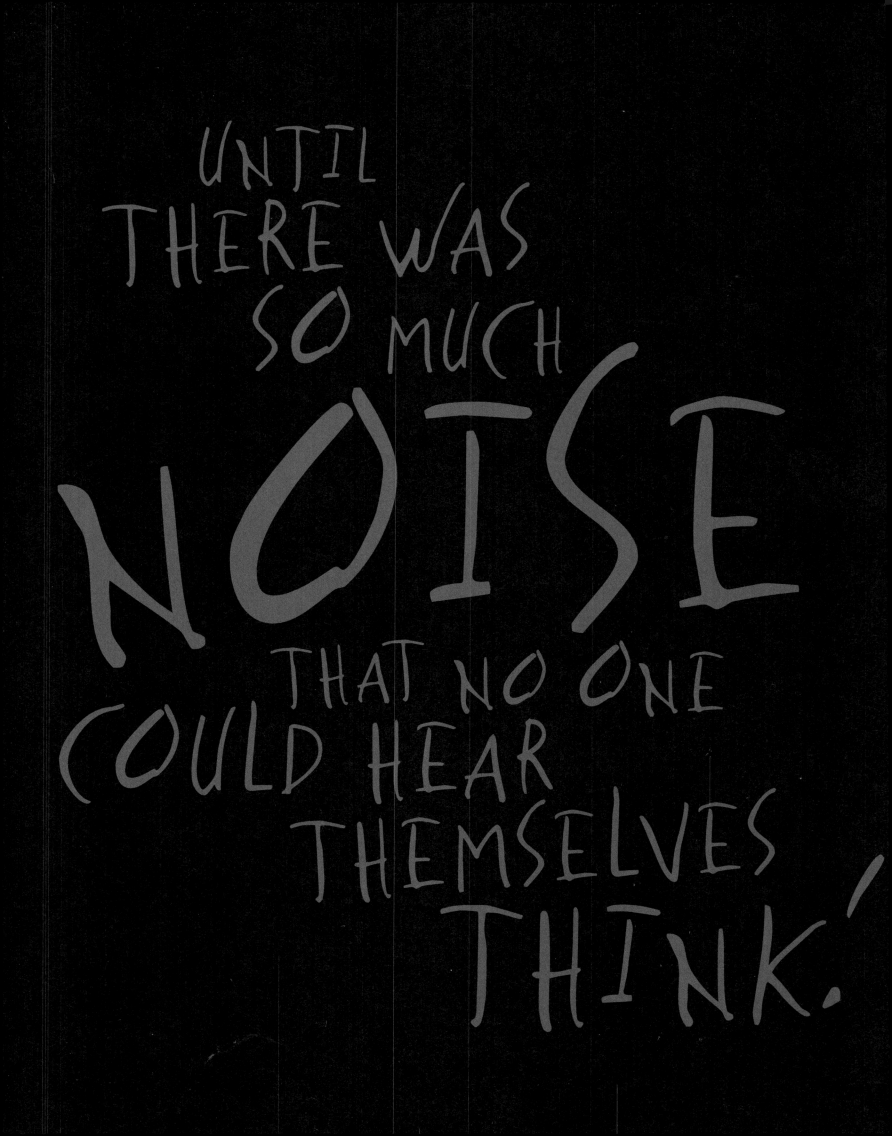

So they stopped thinking.

But in a place high above
the fury of the streets,

someone nurtured
a little piece of
wilderness.

As he
from
his

finding
his
gro

He took his small piece of wilderness . . .

to a place where such small pieces
of wilderness might belong,
and he left all that was important
to him behind.

This final fragment of the wilderness

was carefully gathered in

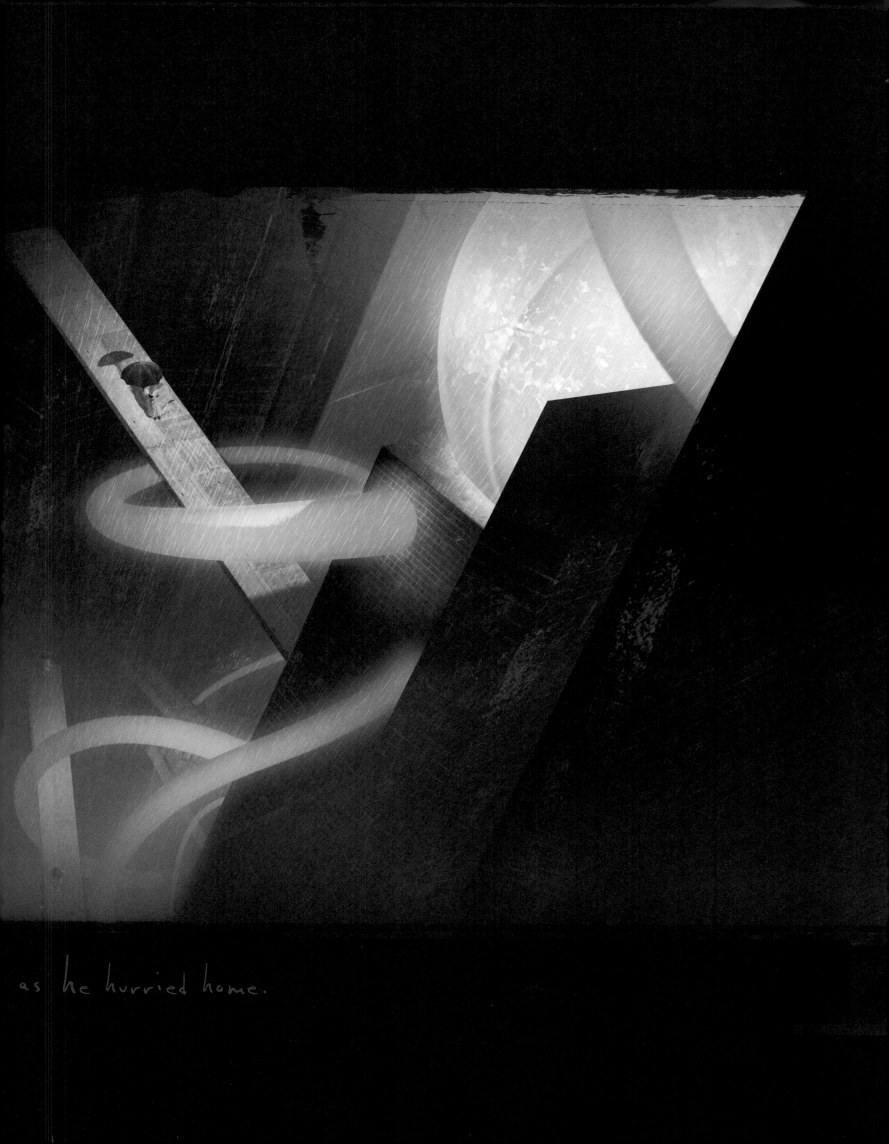

as he hurried home.

Far below,
the crowded streets
and the empty heads
of the OTHERS
fell quiet and still.

But those FEW
warmed hearts watched
as all their hopes and wishes
took to the air
like new seeds
upon the wind.

And in that endless pause...

there came once AGAIN
the sound of bees . . .

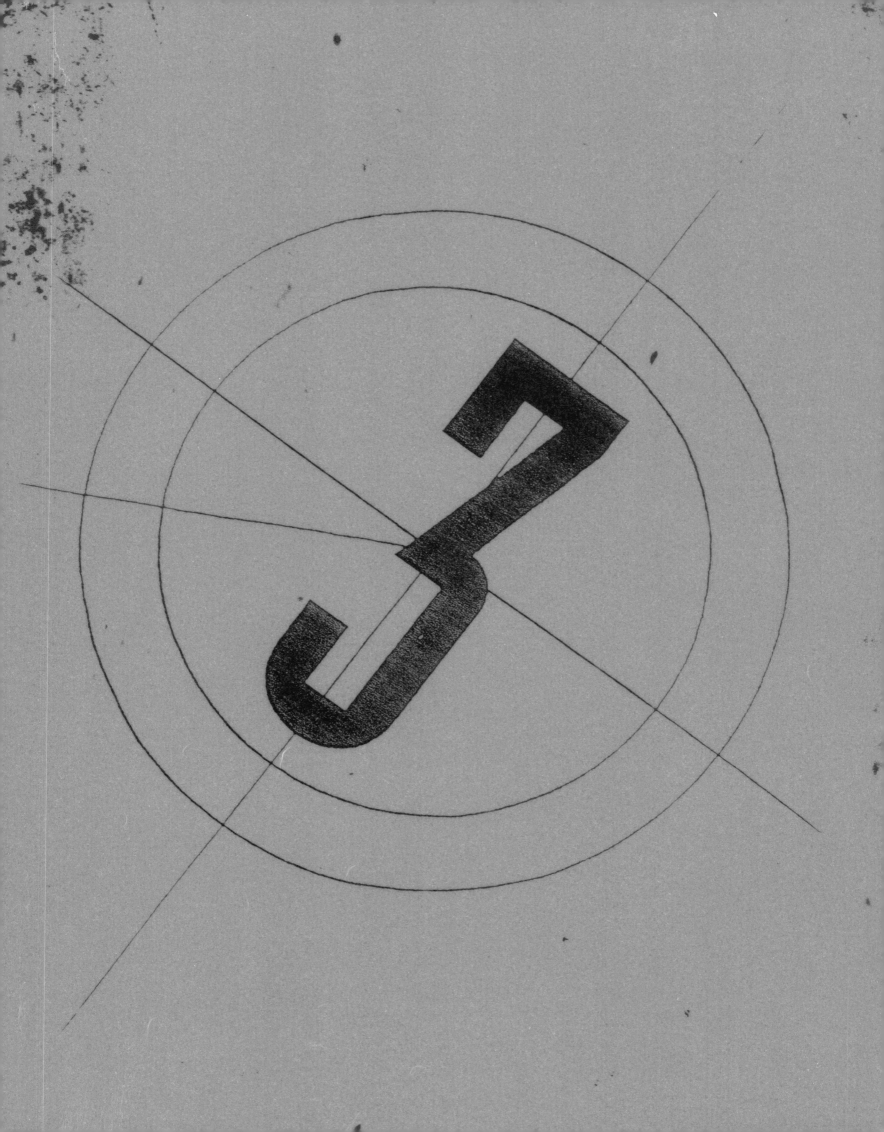

the whispering wind in the wiry grass...

and the song of birds...

in the high blue sky.

The beginning . . .